Daisy and the Egg

Jane Simmons

ORCHARD BOOKS

To my Dad

Orchard Books
96 Leonard Street, London EC2A 4XD
Orchard Books Australia
14 Mars Road, Lane Cove, NSW 2066
1 86039 622 4 (hardback)
1 84121 553 8 (paperback)
First published in Great Britain in 1999
This edition published in 1999
Copyright © Jane Simmons 1999
The right of Jane Simmons to be identified as the author and illustrator of this work has been
asserted by her in accordance with the Copyright, Designs and Patents Act, 1988.
A CIP catalogue record for this book is available from the British Library.
1 2 3 4 5 6 7 8 9 10 (hardback)
1 2 3 4 5 6 7 8 9 10 (paperback)
Printed in Singapore

"How many eggs now?" asked Daisy.
"Four," Auntie Buttercup said proudly,
"my three and Mamma's green one."
"Your Auntie's sitting on an egg for me,"
said Mamma Duck.
"Can I sit on one too?" asked Daisy excitedly.

It wasn't easy.

Every day Mamma Duck
sent Daisy with some food
for Auntie Buttercup.

Daisy listened as the chicks
tapped softly inside their shells.
"You'll have a brother or sister
soon," said Auntie Buttercup.
Daisy was so excited.

When they saw Auntie Buttercup the
next day, she was flapping her wings.
"They're hatching! They're hatching!"
she called.

One duckling had cracked
the shell. Daisy watched her
first cousin struggle out.

"Yuk! It's all wet!" said Daisy.
"Shhh!" scolded Mamma Duck.
Then two more eggs hatched.

While Mamma Duck and Auntie Buttercup talked about names, Daisy waited for Mamma's egg. She thought she heard something . . . but nothing happened.

They all listened . . . but there
was no sound from the egg.

That night Mamma Duck sat on her egg but the next day it still hadn't hatched.

"Some eggs don't. Come and play with your cousins, Daisy," said Mamma Duck.

But Daisy wanted to stay with Mamma's egg.

Daisy made a hole in the feathers,
rolled the egg in and sat on top.
"Come on, Daisy!" called Mamma
Duck. But Daisy wouldn't move.

It was getting dark and Daisy
was cold and tired.

Mamma Duck came back.
"We'll sit together until
morning," she said kindly.
"Yes," said Daisy. . .

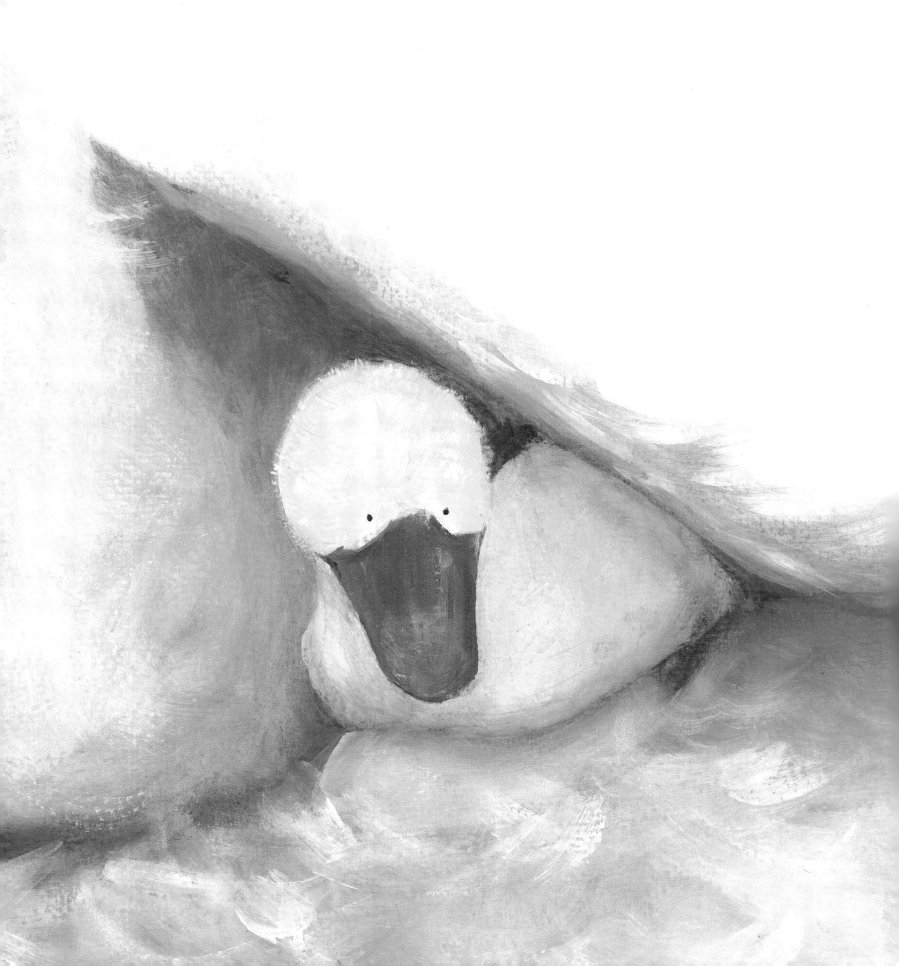

Pip! Pip! Pip! Daisy
woke up. It was the egg!

Her new brother struggled out
of his shell and went "Pip! Pip!"
"Coo!" said Daisy.
"Pip!" he went again.
"Pip!" said Daisy.
"Hello, Pip," said Mamma Duck.

And they all watched
the sun rise on Little Pip's
hatching day.